An Essay on Comedy and the Uses of the Comic Spirit

George Meredith

Pharos Books

ISBN: 978-93-59835-97-6
eISBN: 978-93-59836-51-5

Publisher: Pharos Books (P) Ltd.
Plot No.-55, Main Mother Dairy Road
Pandav Nagar, East Delhi-110092
Phone: 011-40395855, +4049916623
WhatsApp: +91 8368220032
E-mail: sales@pharosbooks.in
Website: www.pharosbooks.in
First Edition: 2024

Printed By: Sushma Book Binding House, Okhla Industrial Area, Phase II, New Delhi-110020

An Essay on Comedy and the Uses of the Comic Spirit
By George Meredith

AN ESSAY ON COMEDY AND THE USES OF THE COMIC SPIRIT by George Meredith

This Essay was first published in 'The New Quarterly Magazine' for April 1877.

ON THE IDEA OF COMEDY AND OF THE USES OF THE COMIC SPIRIT[1]

Good Comedies are such rare productions, that notwithstanding the wealth of our literature in the Comic element, it would not occupy us long to run over the English list. If they are brought to the test I shall propose, very reputable Comedies will be found unworthy of their station, like the ladies of Arthur's Court when they were reduced to the ordeal of the mantle.

There are plain reasons why the Comic poet is not a frequent apparition; and why the great Comic poet remains without a fellow. A society of cultivated men and women is required, wherein ideas are current and the perceptions quick, that he may be supplied with matter and an audience. The semi-barbarism of merely giddy communities, and feverish emotional periods, repel him; and also a state of marked social inequality of the sexes; nor can he whose business is to address the mind be understood where there is not a moderate degree of intellectual activity.

Moreover, to touch and kindle the mind through laughter, demands more than sprightliness, a most subtle delicacy. That must be a natal gift in the Comic poet. The substance he deals with will show him a startling exhibition of the dyer's hand, if he is without it. People are

1. A lecture delivered at the London Institution, February 1st, 1877.

ready to surrender themselves to witty thumps on the back, breast, and sides; all except the head: and it is there that he aims. He must be subtle to penetrate. A corresponding acuteness must exist to welcome him. The necessity for the two conditions will explain how it is that we count him during centuries in the singular number.

'C'est une étrange entreprise que celle de faire rire les honnêtes gens,' Molière says; and the difficulty of the undertaking cannot be over-estimated.

Then again, he is beset with foes to right and left, of a character unknown to the tragic and the lyric poet, or even to philosophers.

We have in this world men whom Rabelais would call agelasts; that is to say, non-laughers; men who are in that respect as dead bodies, which if you prick them do not bleed. The old grey boulder-stone that has finished its peregrination from the rock to the valley, is as easily to be set rolling up again as these men laughing. No collision of circumstances in our mortal career strikes a light for them. It is but one step from being agelastic to misogelastic, and the μισογελως, the laughter-hating, soon learns to dignify his dislike as an objection in morality.

We have another class of men, who are pleased to consider themselves antagonists of the foregoing, and whom we may term hypergelasts; the excessive laughers, ever-laughing, who are as clappers of a bell, that may be rung by a breeze, a grimace; who are so loosely put together that a wink will shake them.

'. . . C'est n'estimer rien qu'estioner tout le monde,'

and to laugh at everything is to have no appreciation of the Comic of Comedy.

Neither of these distinct divisions of non-laughers and over-laughers would be entertained by reading The Rape of the Lock, or seeing a performance of Le Tartuffe. In relation to the stage, they have taken in our land the form and title of Puritan and Bacchanalian. For though the stage is no longer a public offender, and Shakespeare has been revived on it, to give it nobility, we have not yet entirely raised it above the contention of these two parties. Our speaking on the theme of Comedy will appear almost a libertine proceeding to one, while the other will think that the speaking of it seriously brings us into violent contrast with the subject.

Comedy, we have to admit, was never one of the most honoured of the Muses. She was in her origin, short of slaughter, the loudest expression of the little civilization of men. The light of Athene over the head of Achilles illuminates the birth of Greek Tragedy. But Comedy rolled in shouting under the divine protection of the Son of the Wine-jar, as Dionysus is made to proclaim himself by Aristophanes. Our second Charles was the patron, of like benignity, of our Comedy of Manners, which began similarly as a combative performance, under a licence to deride and outrage the Puritan, and was here and there Bacchanalian beyond the Aristophanic example: worse, inasmuch as a cynical licentiousness is more abominable than frank filth. An eminent Frenchman judges from the quality of some of the stuff dredged up for the laughter of men and women who sat through an Athenian Comic play, that they could have had small delicacy in other affairs when they had so little in their choice of entertainment. Perhaps he does not make sufficient allowance for the regulated licence of plain speaking proper to the festival of the god, and claimed by the Comic poet as his inalienable right, or for the fact that it was a festival in a season of licence, in a city accustomed to give ear to the boldest utterance of both sides of a case. However that may be, there can be no question that the men and women who sat through the acting of Wycherley's Country Wife were past blushing. Our tenacity of national impressions has caused the word theatre since then to prod the Puritan nervous system like a satanic instrument; just as one has known Anti-Papists, for whom Smithfield was redolent of a sinister smoke, as though they had a later recollection of the place than the lowing herds. Hereditary Puritanism, regarding the stage, is met, to this day, in many families quite undistinguished by arrogant piety. It has subsided altogether as a power in the profession of morality; but it is an error to suppose it extinct, and unjust also to forget that it had once good reason to hate, shun, and rebuke our public shows.

We shall find ourselves about where the Comic spirit would place us, if we stand at middle distance between the inveterate opponents and the drum-and-fife supporters of Comedy: 'Comme un point fixe fait remarquer l'emportement des autres,' as Pascal says. And were there more in this position, Comic genius would flourish.

Our English idea of a Comedy of Manners might be imaged in the person of a blowsy country girl—say Hoyden, the daughter of Sir Tunbelly Clumsy, who, when at home, 'never disobeyed her father except in the eating of green gooseberries'—transforming to a varnished City madam; with a loud laugh and a mincing step; the crazy ancestress of an accountably fallen descendant. She bustles prodigiously and is punctually smart in her speech, always in a fluster to escape from Dulness, as they say the dogs on the Nile-banks drink at the river running to avoid the crocodile. If the monster catches her, as at times he does, she whips him to a froth, so that those who know Dulness only as a thing of ponderousness, shall fail to recognise him in that light and airy shape.

When she has frolicked through her five Acts to surprise you with the information that Mr. Aimwell is converted by a sudden death in the world outside the scenes into Lord Aimwell, and can marry the lady in the light of day, it is to the credit of her vivacious nature that she does not anticipate your calling her Farce. Five is dignity with a trailing robe; whereas one, two, or three Acts would be short skirts, and degrading. Advice has been given to householders, that they should follow up the shot at a burglar in the dark by hurling the pistol after it, so that if the bullet misses, the weapon may strike and assure the rascal he has it. The point of her wit is in this fashion supplemented by the rattle of her tongue, and effectively, according to the testimony of her admirers. Her wit is at once, like steam in an engine, the motive force and the warning whistle of her headlong course; and it vanishes like the track of steam when she has reached her terminus, never troubling the brains afterwards; a merit that it shares with good wine, to the joy of the Bacchanalians. As to this wit, it is warlike. In the neatest hands it is like the sword of the cavalier in the Mall, quick to flash out upon slight provocation, and for a similar office—to wound. Commonly its attitude is entirely pugilistic; two blunt fists rallying and countering. When harmless, as when the word 'fool' occurs, or allusions to the state of husband, it has the sound of the smack of harlequin's wand upon clown, and is to the same extent exhilarating. Believe that idle empty laughter is the most desirable of recreations, and significant Comedy will seem pale and shallow in comparison. Our popular idea would be hit by the sculptured group of Laughter holding both his sides, while Comedy pummels, by way of tickling him. As to a meaning, she holds that it does not conduce to making merry: you might as well carry cannon on a racing-yacht. Morality is a duenna to be circumvented. This was the view of English Comedy of a sagacious essayist, who said that the end of a Comedy would often be the commencement of a Tragedy, were the curtain to rise again on the performers. In those old days female modesty was protected by a fan, behind which, and it was of a convenient semicircular breadth, the ladies present in the theatre retired at a signal of decorum, to peep, covertly askant, or with the option of so peeping, through a prettily fringed eyelet-hole in the eclipsing arch.

> 'Ego limis specto sic per flabellum clanculum.'—
> TERENCE.

That fan is the flag and symbol of the society giving us our so-called Comedy of Manners, or Comedy of the manners of South-sea Islanders under city veneer; and as to Comic idea, vacuous as the mask without the face behind it.

Elia, whose humour delighted in floating a galleon paradox and wafting it as far as it would go, bewails the extinction of our artificial Comedy, like a poet sighing over the vanished splendour of Cleopatra's Nile-barge; and the sedateness of his plea for a cause condemned even in his time to the penitentiary, is a novel effect of the ludicrous. When the realism of those 'fictitious half-believed personages,' as he calls them, had ceased to strike, they were objectionable company, uncaressable as puppets. Their artifices are staringly naked, and have now the effect of a painted face viewed, after warm hours of dancing, in the morning light. How could the Lurewells and the Plyants ever have been praised for ingenuity in wickedness? Critics, apparently sober, and of high reputation, held up their shallow knaveries for the world to admire. These Lurewells, Plyants, Pinchwifes, Fondlewifes, Miss Prue, Peggy, Hoyden, all of them save charming Milamant, are dead as last year's clothes in a fashionable fine lady's wardrobe, and it must be an exceptionably abandoned Abigail of our period that would look on them with the wish to appear in their likeness. Whether the puppet show of Punch and Judy inspires our street-urchins to have instant recourse to their fists in a dispute, after the fashion of every one of the actors in that public entertainment who gets possession of the cudgel, is open to question: it has been hinted; and angry moralists have traced the national taste for tales of crime to the smell of blood in our nursery-songs. It will at any rate hardly be questioned that it is unwholesome for men and women to see themselves as they are, if they are no better than they should be: and they will not, when they have improved in manners, care much to see themselves as they once were. That comes of realism in the Comic art; and it is not public caprice, but the consequence of a bettering state.[2] The same of an immoral may be said of realistic exhibitions of a vulgar society.

The French make a critical distinction in ***ce qui remue*** from ***ce qui émeut***—that which agitates from that which touches with emotion. In the realistic comedy it is an incessant ***remuage***—no calm, merely bustling figures, and no thought. Excepting Congreve's Way of the World, which failed on the stage, there was nothing to keep our comedy alive on its merits; neither, with all its realism, true portraiture, nor much quotable fun, nor idea; neither salt nor soul.

The French have a school of stately comedy to which they can fly for renovation whenever they have fallen away from it; and their having such a school is mainly the reason why, as John Stuart Mill pointed out, they know men and women more accurately than we do. Molière followed the Horatian precept, to observe the manners of his age and give his characters the colour befitting them at the time. He did not

2. Realism in the writing is carried to such a pitch in THE OLD BACHELOR, that husband and wife use imbecile connubial epithets to one another.

paint in raw realism. He seized his characters firmly for the central purpose of the play, stamped them in the idea, and by slightly raising and softening the object of study (as in the case of the ex-Huguenot, Duke de Montausier,[3] for the study of the Misanthrope, and, according to St. Simon, the Abbe Roquette for Tartuffe), generalized upon it so as to make it permanently human. Concede that it is natural for human creatures to live in society, and Alceste is an imperishable mark of one, though he is drawn in light outline, without any forcible human colouring. Our English school has not clearly imagined society; and of the mind hovering above congregated men and women, it has imagined nothing. The critics who praise it for its downrightness, and for bringing the situations home to us, as they admiringly say, cannot but disapprove of Molière's comedy, which appeals to the individual mind to perceive and participate in the social. We have splendid tragedies, we have the most beautiful of poetic plays, and we have literary comedies passingly pleasant to read, and occasionally to see acted. By literary comedies, I mean comedies of classic inspiration, drawn chiefly from Menander and the Greek New Comedy through Terence; or else comedies of the poet's personal conception, that have had no model in life, and are humorous exaggerations, happy or otherwise. These are the comedies of Ben Jonson, Massinger, and Fletcher. Massinger's Justice Greedy we can all of us refer to a type, 'with fat capon lined' that has been and will be; and he would be comic, as Panurge is comic, but only a Rabelais could set him moving with real animation. Probably Justice Greedy would be comic to the audience of a country booth and to some of our friends. If we have lost our youthful relish for the presentation of characters put together to fit a type, we find it hard to put together the mechanism of a civil smile at his enumeration of his dishes. Something of the same is to be said of Bobadil, swearing 'by the foot of Pharaoh'; with a reservation, for he is made to move faster, and to act. The comic of Jonson is a scholar's excogitation of the comic; that of Massinger a moralist's.

3. Tallemant des Réaux, in his rough portrait of the Duke, shows the foundation of the character of Alceste.

Shakespeare is a well-spring of characters which are saturated with the comic spirit; with more of what we will call blood-life than is to be found anywhere out of Shakespeare; and they are of this world, but they are of the world enlarged to our embrace by imagination, and by great poetic imagination. They are, as it were—I put it to suit my present comparison—creatures of the woods and wilds, not in walled towns, not grouped and toned to pursue a comic exhibition of the narrower world of society. Jaques, Falstaff and his regiment, the varied troop of Clowns, Malvolio, Sir Hugh Evans and Fluellen—marvellous Welshmen!—Benedict and Beatrice, Dogberry, and the rest, are subjects of a special study in the poetically comic.

His Comedy of incredible imbroglio belongs to the literary section. One may conceive that there was a natural resemblance between him and Menander, both in the scheme and style of his lighter plays. Had Shakespeare lived in a later and less emotional, less heroical period of our history, he might have turned to the painting of manners as well as humanity. Euripides would probably, in the time of Menander, when Athens was enslaved but prosperous, have lent his hand to the composition of romantic comedy. He certainly inspired that fine genius.

Politically it is accounted a misfortune for France that her nobles thronged to the Court of Louis Quatorze. It was a boon to the comic poet. He had that lively quicksilver world of the animalcule passions, the huge pretensions, the placid absurdities, under his eyes in full activity; vociferous quacks and snapping dupes, hypocrites, posturers, extravagants, pedants, rose-pink ladies and mad grammarians, sonneteering marquises, high-flying mistresses, plain-minded maids, inter-threading as in a loom, noisy as at a fair. A simply bourgeois circle will not furnish it, for the middle class must have the brilliant, flippant, independent upper for a spur and a pattern; otherwise it is likely to be inwardly dull as well as outwardly correct. Yet, though the King was benevolent toward Molière, it is not to the French Court that we are indebted for his unrivalled studies of mankind in society. For the amusement of the Court the ballets and farces were written, which are dearer to the rabble upper, as to the rabble lower, class than intellectual comedy. The French bourgeoisie of Paris were sufficiently quick-witted and enlightened by education to welcome great works like Le Tartuffe, Les Femmes Savantes, and Le Misanthrope, works that were perilous ventures on the popular intelligence, big vessels to launch on streams running to shallows. The Tartuffe hove into view as an enemy's vessel; it offended, not ***Dieu mais les dévots***, as the Prince de Condé explained the cabal raised against it to the King.

The Femmes Savantes is a capital instance of the uses of comedy in teaching the world to understand what ails it. The farce of the Précieuses ridiculed and put a stop to the monstrous romantic jargon made popular by certain famous novels. The comedy of the Femmes Savantes exposed the later and less apparent but more finely comic absurdity of an excessive purism in grammar and diction, and the tendency to be idiotic in precision. The French had felt the burden of this new nonsense; but they had to see the comedy several times before they were consoled in their suffering by seeing the cause of it exposed.

The Misanthrope was yet more frigidly received. Molière thought it dead. 'I cannot improve on it, and assuredly never shall,' he said. It is one of the French titles to honour that this quintessential comedy of the opposition of Alceste and Célimène was ultimately understood and applauded. In all countries the middle class presents the public which, fighting the world, and with a good footing in the fight, knows the world best. It may be the most selfish, but that is a question leading us into sophistries. Cultivated men and women, who do not skim the cream of life, and are attached to the duties, yet escape the harsher blows, make acute and balanced observers. Molière is their poet.

Of this class in England, a large body, neither Puritan nor Bacchanalian, have a sentimental objection to face the study of the actual world. They take up disdain of it, when its truths appear humiliating: when the facts are not immediately forced on them, they take up the pride of incredulity. They live in a hazy atmosphere that they suppose an ideal one. Humorous writing they will endure, perhaps approve, if it mingles with pathos to shake and elevate the feelings. They approve of Satire, because, like the beak of the vulture, it smells of carrion, which they are not. But of Comedy they have a shivering dread, for Comedy enfolds them with the wretched host of the world, huddles them with us all in an ignoble assimilation, and cannot be used by any exalted variety as a scourge and a broom. Nay, to be an exalted variety is to come under the calm curious eye of the Comic spirit, and be probed for what you are. Men are seen among them, and very many cultivated women. You may distinguish them by a favourite phrase: 'Surely we are not so bad!' and the remark: 'If that is human nature, save us from it!' as if it could be done: but in the peculiar Paradise of the wilful people who will not see, the exclamation assumes the saving grace.

Yet should you ask them whether they dislike sound sense, they vow they do not. And question cultivated women whether it pleases them to be shown moving on an intellectual level with men, they will answer that it does; numbers of them claim the situation. Now, Comedy is the fountain of sound sense; not the less perfectly sound on account of the sparkle: and Comedy lifts women to a station offering them free play for their wit, as they usually show it, when they have it, on the side of sound sense. The higher the Comedy, the more prominent the part they enjoy in it. Dorine in the Tartuffe is common-sense incarnate, though palpably a waiting-maid. Célimène is undisputed mistress of the same attribute in the Misanthrope; wiser as a woman than Alceste as man. In Congreve's Way of the World, Millamant overshadows Mirabel, the sprightliest male figure of English comedy.

But those two ravishing women, so copious and so choice of speech, who fence with men and pass their guard, are heartless! Is it not preferable to be the pretty idiot, the passive beauty, the adorable bundle of caprices, very feminine, very sympathetic, of romantic and sentimental fiction? Our women are taught to think so. The Agnès of the École des Femmes should be a lesson for men. The heroines of Comedy are like women of the world, not necessarily heartless from being clear-sighted: they seem so to the sentimentally-reared only for the reason that they use their wits, and are not wandering vessels crying for a captain or a pilot. Comedy is an exhibition of their battle with men, and that of men with them: and as the two, however divergent, both look on one object, namely, Life, the gradual similarity of their impressions must bring them to some resemblance. The Comic poet dares to show us men and women coming to this mutual likeness; he is for saying that when they draw together in social life their minds grow liker; just as the philosopher discerns the similarity of boy and girl, until the girl is marched away to the nursery. Philosopher and Comic poet are of a cousinship in the eye they cast on life: and they are equally unpopular with our wilful English of the hazy region and the ideal that is not to be disturbed.

Thus, for want of instruction in the Comic idea, we lose a large audience among our cultivated middle class that we should expect to support Comedy. The sentimentalist is as averse as the Puritan and as the Bacchanalian.

Our traditions are unfortunate. The public taste is with the idle laughers, and still inclines to follow them. It may be shown by an analysis of Wycherley's Plain Dealer, a coarse prose adaption of the Misanthrope, stuffed with lumps of realism in a vulgarized theme to hit the mark of English appetite, that we have in it the keynote of the Comedy of our stage. It is Molière travestied, with the hoof to his foot and hair on the pointed tip of his ear. And how difficult it is for writers to disentangle themselves from bad traditions is noticeable when we find Goldsmith, who had grave command of the Comic in narrative, producing an elegant farce for a Comedy; and Fielding, who was a master of the Comic both in narrative and in dialogue, not even approaching to the presentable in farce.

These bad traditions of Comedy affect us not only on the stage, but in our literature, and may be tracked into our social life. They are the ground of the heavy moralizings by which we are outwearied, about Life as a Comedy, and Comedy as a jade,[4] when popular writers, conscious of fatigue in creativeness, desire to be cogent in a modish cynicism:

---

4. See Tom Jones, book viii. chapter I, for Fielding's opinion of our Comedy. But he puts it simply; not as an exercise in the quasi-philosophical bathetic.

perversions of the idea of life, and of the proper esteem for the society we have wrested from brutishness, and would carry higher. Stock images of this description are accepted by the timid and the sensitive, as well as by the saturnine, quite seriously; for not many look abroad with their own eyes, fewer still have the habit of thinking for themselves. Life, we know too well, is not a Comedy, but something strangely mixed; nor is Comedy a vile mask. The corrupted importation from France was noxious; a noble entertainment spoilt to suit the wretched taste of a villanous age; and the later imitations of it, partly drained of its poison and made decorous, became tiresome, notwithstanding their fun, in the perpetual recurring of the same situations, owing to the absence of original study and vigour of conception. Scene v. Act 2 of the Misanthrope, owing, no doubt, to the fact of our not producing matter for original study, is repeated in succession by Wycherley, Congreve, and Sheridan, and as it is at second hand, we have it done cynically—or such is the tone; in the manner of 'below stairs.' Comedy thus treated may be accepted as a version of the ordinary worldly understanding of our social life; at least, in accord with the current dicta concerning it. The epigrams can be made; but it is uninstructive, rather tending to do disservice. Comedy justly treated, as you find it in Molière, whom we so clownishly mishandled, the Comedy of Molière throws no infamous reflection upon life. It is deeply conceived, in the first place, and therefore it cannot be impure. Meditate on that statement. Never did man wield so shrieking a scourge upon vice, but his consummate self-mastery is not shaken while administering it. Tartuffe and Harpagon, in fact, are made each to whip himself and his class, the false pietists, and the insanely covetous. Molière has only set them in motion. He strips Folly to the skin, displays the imposture of the creature, and is content to offer her better clothing, with the lesson Chrysale reads to Philaminte and Bélise. He conceives purely, and he writes purely, in the simplest language, the simplest of French verse. The source of his wit is clear reason: it is a fountain of that soil; and it springs to vindicate reason, common-sense, rightness and justice; for no vain purpose ever. The wit is of such pervading spirit that it inspires a pun with meaning and interest.[5] His moral does not hang like a tail, or preach from one character incessantly cocking an eye at the audience, as in recent realistic French Plays: but is in the heart of his work, throbbing with every pulsation of an organic structure. If Life is likened to the comedy of Molière, there is no scandal in the comparison.

Congreve's Way of the World is an exception to our other comedies, his own among them, by virtue of the remarkable brilliancy of the writing, and the figure of Millamant. The comedy has no idea in it, beyond the stale one, that so the world goes; and it concludes with the jaded discovery of a document at a convenient season for the descent of the curtain. A plot was an afterthought with Congreve. By the help of a wooden villain (Maskwell) marked Gallows to the flattest eye, he gets a sort of plot in The Double Dealer.[6] His Way of the World might be called The Conquest of a Town Coquette, and Millamant is a perfect portrait of a coquette, both in her resistance to Mirabel and the manner of her surrender, and also in her tongue. The wit here is not so salient as in certain passages of Love for Love, where Valentine feigns madness or retorts on his father, or Mrs. Frail rejoices in the harmlessness of wounds to a woman's virtue, if she 'keeps them from air.' In The Way of the World, it appears less prepared in the smartness, and is more diffused in the more characteristic style of the speakers. Here, however, as elsewhere, his famous wit is like a bully-fencer, not ashamed to lay traps for its exhibition, transparently petulant for the train between certain ordinary words and the powder-magazine of the improprieties to be fired. Contrast the wit of Congreve with Molière's. That of the first is a Toledo blade, sharp, and wonderfully supple for

5. Femmes Savantes:

   BÉLISE: Veux-tu toute la vie offenser la grammaire?

   MARTINE: Qui parle d'offenser grand'mère ni grand-père?'

   The pun is delivered in all sincerity, from the mouth of a rustic.

6. Maskwell seems to have been carved on the model of Iago, as by the hand of an enterprising urchin. He apostrophizes his 'invention' repeatedly. 'Thanks, my invention.' He hits on an invention, to say: 'Was it my brain or Providence? no matter which.' It is no matter which, but it was not his brain.

steel; cast for duelling, restless in the scabbard, being so pretty when out of it. To shine, it must have an adversary. Molière's wit is like a running brook, with innumerable fresh lights on it at every turn of the wood through which its business is to find a way. It does not run in search of obstructions, to be noisy over them; but when dead leaves and viler substances are heaped along the course, its natural song is heightened. Without effort, and with no dazzling flashes of achievement, it is full of healing, the wit of good breeding, the wit of wisdom.

'Genuine humour and true wit,' says Landor,[7] 'require a sound and capacious mind, which is always a grave one. Rabelais and La Fontaine are recorded by their countrymen to have been ***rêveurs***. Few men have been graver than Pascal. Few men have been wittier.'

To apply the citation of so great a brain as Pascal's to our countryman would be unfair. Congreve had a certain soundness of mind; of capacity, in the sense intended by Landor, he had little. Judging him by his wit, he performed some happy thrusts, and taking it for genuine, it is a surface wit, neither rising from a depth nor flowing from a spring.

'On voit qu'il se travaille à dire de bons mots.'

He drives the poor hack word, 'fool,' as cruelly to the market for wit as any of his competitors. Here is an example, that has been held up for eulogy:

WITWOUD: He has brought me a letter from the fool my brother, etc. etc.

MIRABEL: A fool, and your brother, Witwoud?

WITWOUD: Ay, ay, my half-brother. My half-brother he is; no nearer, upon my honour.

MIRABEL: Then 'tis possible he may be but half a fool.

By evident preparation. This is a sort of wit one remembers to have heard at school, of a brilliant outsider; perhaps to have been guilty of oneself, a trifle later. It was, no doubt, a blaze of intellectual fireworks to the bumpkin squire, who came to London to go to the theatre and learn manners.

7. Imaginary Conversations: Alfieri and the Jew Salomon.

Where Congreve excels all his English rivals is in his literary force, and a succinctness of style peculiar to him. He had correct judgement, a correct ear, readiness of illustration within a narrow range, in snapshots of the obvious at the obvious, and copious language. He hits the mean of a fine style and a natural in dialogue. He is at once precise and voluble. If you have ever thought upon style you will acknowledge it to be a signal accomplishment. In this he is a classic, and is worthy of treading a measure with Molière. The Way of the World may be read out currently at a first glance, so sure are the accents of the emphatic meaning to strike the eye, perforce of the crispness and cunning polish of the sentences. You have not to look over them before you confide yourself to him; he will carry you safe. Sheridan imitated, but was far from surpassing him. The flow of boudoir Billingsgate in Lady Wishfort is unmatched for the vigour and pointedness of the tongue. It spins along with a final ring, like the voice of Nature in a fury, and is, indeed, racy eloquence of the elevated fishwife.

Millamant is an admirable, almost a lovable heroine. It is a piece of genius in a writer to make a woman's manner of speech portray her. You feel sensible of her presence in every line of her speaking. The stipulations with her lover in view of marriage, her fine lady's delicacy, and fine lady's easy evasions of indelicacy, coquettish airs, and playing with irresolution, which in a common maid would be bashfulness, until she submits to 'dwindle into a wife,' as she says, form a picture that lives in the frame, and is in harmony with Mirabel's description of her:

'Here she comes, i' faith, full sail, with her fan spread, and her streamers out, and a shoal of fools for tenders.'

And, after an interview:

'Think of you! To think of a whirlwind, though 'twere in a whirlwind, were a case of more steady contemplation, a very tranquillity of mind and mansion.'

There is a picturesqueness, as of Millamant and no other, in her voice, when she is encouraged to take Mirabel by Mrs. Fainall, who is 'sure she has a mind to him':

MILLAMANT: Are you? I think I have—and the horrid man looks as if he thought so too, etc. etc.

One hears the tones, and sees the sketch and colour of the whole scene in reading it.

Célimène is behind Millamant in vividness. An air of bewitching whimsicality hovers over the graces of this Comic heroine, like the lively conversational play of a beautiful mouth.

But in wit she is no rival of Célimène. What she utters adds to her personal witchery, and is not further memorable. She is a flashing portrait, and a type of the superior ladies who do not think, not of those who do. In representing a class, therefore, it is a lower class, in the proportion that one of Gainsborough's full-length aristocratic women is below the permanent impressiveness of a fair Venetian head.

Millamant side by side with Célimène is an example of how far the realistic painting of a character can be carried to win our favour; and of where it falls short. Célimène is a woman's mind in movement, armed with an ungovernable wit; with perspicacious clear eyes for the world, and a very distinct knowledge that she belongs to the world, and is most at home in it. She is attracted to Alceste by her esteem for his honesty; she cannot avoid seeing where the good sense of the man is diseased.

Rousseau, in his letter to D'Alembert on the subject of the Misanthrope, discusses the character of Alceste, as though Molière had put him forth for an absolute example of misanthropy; whereas Alceste is only a misanthrope of the circle he finds himself placed in: he has a touching faith in the virtue residing in the country, and a critical love of sweet simpleness. Nor is he the principal person of the comedy to which he gives a name. He is only passively comic. Célimène is the active spirit. While he is denouncing and railing, the trial is imposed upon her to make the best of him, and control herself, as much as a witty woman, eagerly courted, can do. By appreciating him she practically confesses her faultiness, and she is better disposed to meet him half-way than he is to bend an inch: only she is ***une âme***

de vingt ans, the world is pleasant, and if the gilded flies of the Court are silly, uncompromising fanatics have their ridiculous features as well. Can she abandon the life they make agreeable to her, for a man who will not be guided by the common sense of his class; and who insists on plunging into one extreme—equal to suicide in her eyes—to avoid another? That is the comic question of the Misanthrope. Why will he not continue to mix with the world smoothly, appeased by the flattery of her secret and really sincere preference of him, and taking his revenge in satire of it, as she does from her own not very lofty standard, and will by and by do from his more exalted one?

Célimène is worldliness: Alceste is unworldliness. It does not quite imply unselfishness; and that is perceived by her shrewd head. Still he is a very uncommon figure in her circle, and she esteems him, ***l'homme aux rubans verts***, 'who sometimes diverts but more often horribly vexes her,' as she can say of him when her satirical tongue is on the run. Unhappily the soul of truth in him, which wins her esteem, refuses to be tamed, or silent, or unsuspicious, and is the perpetual obstacle to their good accord. He is that melancholy person, the critic of everybody save himself; intensely sensitive to the faults of others, wounded by them; in love with his own indubitable honesty, and with his ideal of the simpler form of life befitting it: qualities which constitute the satirist. He is a Jean Jacques of the Court. His proposal to Célimène when he pardons her, that she should follow him in flying humankind, and his frenzy of detestation of her at her refusal, are thoroughly in the mood of Jean Jacques. He is an impracticable creature of a priceless virtue; but Célimène may feel that to fly with him to the desert: that is from the Court to the country

'Où d'être homme d'honneur on ait la liberté,'

she is likely to find herself the companion of a starving satirist, like that poor princess who ran away with the waiting-man, and when both were hungry in the forest, was ordered to give him flesh. She is a ***fieffée*** coquette, rejoicing in her wit and her attractions, and distinguished by her inclination for Alceste in the midst of her many other lovers; only she finds it hard to cut them off—what woman with a train does not?—and when the exposure of her naughty wit has laid her under their rebuke, she will do the utmost she can: she will give her hand to honesty, but she cannot quite abandon worldliness. She would be unwise if she did.

The fable is thin. Our pungent contrivers of plots would see no indication of life in the outlines. The life of the comedy is in the idea. As with the singing of the sky-lark out of sight, you must love the bird to be attentive to the song, so in this highest flight of the Comic Muse, you must love pure Comedy warmly to understand the Misanthrope: you must be receptive of the idea of Comedy. And to love Comedy you must know the real world, and know men and women well enough not to expect too much of them, though you may still hope for good.

Menander wrote a comedy called Misogynes, said to have been the most celebrated of his works. This misogynist is a married man, according to the fragment surviving, and is a hater of women through hatred of his wife. He generalizes upon them from the example of this lamentable adjunct of his fortunes, and seems to have got the worst of it in the contest with her, which is like the issue in reality, in the polite world. He seems also to have deserved it, which may be as true to the copy. But we are unable to say whether the wife was a good voice of her sex: or how far Menander in this instance raised the idea of woman from the mire it was plunged into by the comic poets, or rather satiric dramatists, of the middle period of Greek Comedy preceding him and the New Comedy, who devoted their wit chiefly to the abuse, and for a diversity, to the eulogy of extra-mural ladies of conspicuous fame. Menander idealized them without purposely elevating. He satirized a certain Thais, and his Thais of the Eunuchus of Terence is neither professionally attractive nor repulsive; his picture of the two Andrians, Chrysis and her sister, is nowhere to be matched for tenderness. But the condition of honest women in his day did not permit of the freedom of action and fencing dialectic of a Célimène, and consequently it is below our mark of pure Comedy.

Sainte-Beuve conjures up the ghost of Menander, saying: For the love of me love Terence. It is through love of Terence that moderns are able to love Menander; and what is preserved of Terence has not apparently given us the best of the friend of Epicurus. ?ισο?μενος the lover taken in horror, and Περικειρομενη the damsel shorn of her locks, have a promising sound for scenes of jealousy and a too masterful display of lordly authority, leading to regrets, of the kind known to intemperate men who imagined they were fighting with the weaker, as the fragments indicate.

Of the six comedies of Terence, four are derived from Menander; two, the Hecyra and the Phormio, from Apollodorus. These two are inferior in comic action and the peculiar sweetness of Menander to the Andria, the Adelphi, the Heautontimorumenus, and the Eunuchus: but Phormio is a more dashing and amusing convivial parasite than the Gnatho of the last-named comedy. There were numerous rivals of whom we know next to nothing—except by the quotations of Athenæus and Plutarch, and the Greek grammarians who cited them to support a dictum—in this as in the preceding periods of comedy in Athens, for Menander's plays are counted by many scores, and they were crowned by the prize only eight times. The favourite poet with critics, in Greece as in Rome, was Menander; and if some of his rivals here and there surpassed him in comic force, and out-stripped him in competition by an appositeness to the occasion that had previously in the same way deprived the genius of Aristophanes of its due reward in Clouds and Birds, his position as chief of the comic poets of his age was unchallenged. Plutarch very unnecessarily drags Aristophanes into a comparison with him, to the confusion of the older poet. Their aims, the matter they dealt in, and the times, were quite dissimilar. But it is no wonder that Plutarch, writing when Athenian beauty of style was the delight of his patrons, should rank Menander at the highest. In what degree of faithfulness Terence copied Menander, whether, as he states of the passage in the Adelphi taken from Diphilus, ***verbum de verbo*** in the lovelier scenes—the description of the last words of the dying Andrian, and of her funeral, for instance—remains conjectural. For us Terence shares with his master the praise of an amenity that is like Elysian speech, equable and ever gracious; like the face of the Andrian's young sister:

'Adeo modesto, adeo venusto, ut nihil supra.'

The celebrated 'flens quam familiariter,' of which the closest rendering grounds hopelessly on harsh prose, to express the sorrowful confidingness of a young girl who has lost her sister and dearest friend, and has but her lover left to her; 'she turned and flung herself on his bosom, weeping as though at home there': this our instinct tells us must be Greek, though hardly finer in Greek. Certain lines of Terence, compared with the original fragments, show that he embellished them; but his taste was too exquisite for him to do other than devote his genius to the honest translation of such pieces as the above. Menander, then; with him, through the affinity of sympathy, Terence; and Shakespeare and Molière have this beautiful translucency of language: and the study of the comic poets might be recommended, if for that only.

A singular ill fate befell the writings of Menander. What we have of him in Terence was chosen probably to please the cultivated Romans;[8] and is a romantic play with a comic intrigue, obtained in two instances, the Andria and the Eunuchus, by rolling a couple of his originals into one. The titles of certain of the lost plays indicate the comic illumining character; a Self-pitier, a Self-chastiser, an Ill-tempered man, a Superstitious, an Incredulous, etc., point to suggestive domestic themes.

Terence forwarded manuscript translations from Greece, that suffered shipwreck; he, who could have restored the treasure, died on the way home. The zealots of Byzantium completed the work of destruction. So we have the four comedies of Terence, numbering six of Menander, with a few sketches of plots—one of them, the

8. Terence did not please the rough old conservative Romans; they liked Plautus better, and the recurring mention of the vetus poeta in his prologues, who plagued him with the crusty critical view of his productions, has in the end a comic effect on the reader.

Thesaurus, introduces a miser, whom we should have liked to contrast with Harpagon—and a multitude of small fragments of a sententious cast, fitted for quotation. Enough remains to make his greatness felt.

Without undervaluing other writers of Comedy, I think it may be said that Menander and Molière stand alone specially as comic poets of the feelings and the idea. In each of them there is a conception of the Comic that refines even to pain, as in the Menedemus of the Heautontimorumenus, and in the Misanthrope. Menander and Molière have given the principal types to Comedy hitherto. The Micio and Demea of the Adelphi, with their opposing views of the proper management of youth, are still alive; the Sganarelles and Arnolphes of the École des Maris and the École des Femmes, are not all buried. Tartuffe is the father of the hypocrites; Orgon of the dupes; Thraso, of the braggadocios; Alceste of the 'Manlys'; Davus and Syrus of the intriguing valets, the Scapins and Figaros. Ladies that soar in the realms of Rose-Pink, whose language wears the nodding plumes of intellectual conceit, are traceable to Philaminte and Bélise of the Femmes Savantes: and the mordant witty women have the tongue of Célimène. The reason is, that these two poets idealized upon life: the foundation of their types is real and in the quick, but they painted with spiritual strength, which is the solid in Art.

The idealistic conceptions of Comedy gives breadth and opportunities of daring to Comic genius, and helps to solve the difficulties it creates. How, for example, shall an audience be assured that an evident and monstrous dupe is actually deceived without being an absolute fool? In Le Tartuffe the note of high Comedy strikes when Orgon on his return home hears of his idol's excellent appetite. '***Le pauvre homme***!' he exclaims. He is told that the wife of his bosom has been unwell. '***Et Tartuffe***?' he asks, impatient to hear him spoken of, his mind suffused with the thought of Tartuffe, crazy with tenderness, and again he croons, '***Le pauvre homme***!' It is the mother's cry of pitying delight at a nurse's recital of the feats in young animal gluttony of her cherished infant. After this masterstroke of the Comic, you not only put faith in Orgon's roseate prepossession, you share it with him by comic sympathy, and can listen with no more than a tremble of the laughing muscles to the instance he gives of the sublime humanity of Tartuffe:

> 'Un rien presque suffit pour le scandaliser,
> Jusque-là, qu'il se vint l'autre jour accuser
> D'avoir pris une puce en faisant sa prière,
> Et de l'avoir tuée avec trop de colère.'

And to have killed it too wrathfully! Translating Molière is like humming an air one has heard performed by an accomplished violinist of the pure tones without flourish.

Orgon, awakening to find another dupe in Madame Pernelle, incredulous of the revelations which have at last opened his own besotted eyes, is a scene of the double Comic, vivified by the spell previously cast on the mind. There we feel the power of the poet's creation; and in the sharp light of that sudden turn the humanity is livelier than any realistic work can make it.

Italian Comedy gives many hints for a Tartuffe; but they may be found in Boccaccio, as well as in Machiavelli's Mandragola. The Frate Timoteo of this piece is only a very oily friar, compliantly assisting an intrigue with ecclesiastical sophisms (to use the mildest word) for payment. Frate Timoteo has a fine Italian priestly pose.

DONNA: Credete voi, che'l Turco passi questo anno in Italia?

F. TIM.: Se voi non fate orazione, si.

Priestly arrogance and unctuousness, and trickeries and casuistries, cannot be painted without our discovering a likeness in the long Italian gallery. Goldoni sketched the Venetian manners of the decadence of the Republic with a French pencil, and was an Italian Scribe in style.

The Spanish stage is richer in such Comedies as that which furnished the idea of the Menteur to Corneille. But you must force yourself to believe that this liar is not forcing his vein when he piles lie upon lie. There is no preceding touch to win the mind to credulity.

Spanish Comedy is generally in sharp outline, as of skeletons; in quick movement, as of marionnettes. The Comedy might be performed by a troop of the ***corps de ballet***; and in the recollection of the reading it resolves to an animated shuffle of feet. It is, in fact, something other than the true idea of Comedy. Where the sexes are separated, men and women grow, as the Portuguese call it, ***affaimados*** of one another, famine-stricken; and all the tragic elements are on the stage. Don Juan is a comic character that sends souls flying: nor does the humour of the breaking of a dozen women's hearts conciliate the Comic Muse with the drawing of blood.

German attempts at Comedy remind one vividly of Heine's image of his country in the dancing of Atta Troll. Lessing tried his hand at it, with a sobering effect upon readers. The intention to produce the reverse effect is just visible, and therein, like the portly graces of the poor old Pyrenean Bear poising and twirling on his right hind-leg and his left, consists the fun. Jean Paul Richter gives the best edition of the German Comic in the contrast of Siebenkäs with his Lenette. A light of the Comic is in Goethe; enough to complete the splendid figure of the man, but no more.

The German literary laugh, like the timed awakenings of their Barbarossa in the hollows of the Untersberg, is infrequent, and rather monstrous—never a laugh of men and women in concert. It comes of unrefined abstract fancy, grotesque or grim, or gross, like the peculiar humours of their little earthmen. Spiritual laughter they have not yet attained to: sentimentalism waylays them in the flight. Here and there a Volkslied or Märchen shows a national aptitude for stout animal laughter; and we see that the literature is built on it, which is hopeful so far; but to enjoy it, to enter into the philosophy of the Broad Grin, that seems to hesitate between the skull and the embryo, and reaches its perfection in breadth from the pulling of two square fingers at the corners of the mouth, one must have aid of 'the good Rhine wine,' and be of German blood unmixed besides. This treble-Dutch lumbersomeness of the Comic spirit is of itself exclusive of the idea of Comedy, and the poor voice allowed to women in German domestic life will account for the absence of comic dialogues reflecting upon life in that land. I shall speak of it again in the second section of this lecture.

Eastward you have total silence of Comedy among a people intensely susceptible to laughter, as the Arabian Nights will testify. Where the veil is over women's-faces, you cannot have society, without which the senses are barbarous and the Comic spirit is driven to the gutters of grossness to slake its thirst. Arabs in this respect are worse than Italians—much worse than Germans; just in the degree that their system of treating women is worse.

M. Saint-Marc Girardin, the excellent French essayist and master of critical style, tells of a conversation he had once with an Arab gentleman on the topic of the different management of these difficult creatures in Orient and in Occident: and the Arab spoke in praise of many good results of the greater freedom enjoyed by Western ladies, and the charm of conversing with them. He was questioned why his countrymen took no measures to grant them something of that kind of liberty. He jumped out of his individuality in a twinkling, and entered into the sentiments of his race, replying, from the pinnacle of a splendid conceit, with affected humility of manner: '***You*** can look on them without perturbation—but ***we***!' . . . And after this profoundly comic interjection, he added, in deep tones, 'The very face of a woman!' Our representative of temperate notions demurely consented that the Arab's pride of inflammability should insist on the prudery of the veil as the civilizing medium of his race.

There has been fun in Bagdad. But there never will be civilization where Comedy is not possible; and that comes of some degree of social equality of the sexes. I am not quoting the Arab to exhort and disturb the somnolent East; rather for cultivated women to recognize that the Comic Muse is one of their best friends. They are blind to their interests in swelling the ranks of the sentimentalists. Let them look with their clearest vision abroad and at home. They will see that where they have no social freedom, Comedy is absent: where they are household drudges, the form of Comedy is primitive: where they are tolerably independent, but uncultivated, exciting melodrama takes its place and a sentimental version of them. Yet the Comic will out, as they would know if they listened to some of the private conversations of men whose minds are undirected by the Comic Muse: as the sentimental man, to his astonishment, would know likewise, if he in similar fashion could receive a lesson. But where women are on the road to an equal footing with men, in attainments and in liberty—in what they have won for themselves, and what has been granted them by a fair civilization—there, and only waiting to be transplanted from life to the stage, or the novel, or the poem, pure Comedy flourishes, and is, as it would help them to be, the sweetest of diversions, the wisest of delightful companions.

Now, to look about us in the present time, I think it will be acknowledged that in neglecting the cultivation of the Comic idea, we are losing the aid of a powerful auxiliar. You see Folly perpetually sliding into new shapes in a society possessed of wealth and leisure, with many whims, many strange ailments and strange doctors. Plenty of common-sense is in the world to thrust her back when she pretends to empire. But the first-born of common-sense, the vigilant Comic, which is the genius of thoughtful laughter, which would readily extinguish her at the outset, is not serving as a public advocate.

You will have noticed the disposition of common-sense, under pressure of some pertinacious piece of light-headedness, to grow impatient and angry. That is a sign of the absence, or at least of the dormancy, of the Comic idea. For Folly is the natural prey of the Comic, known to it in all her transformations, in every disguise; and it is with the springing delight of hawk over heron, hound after fox, that it gives her chase, never fretting, never tiring, sure of having her, allowing her no rest.

Contempt is a sentiment that cannot be entertained by comic intelligence. What is it but an excuse to be idly minded, or personally lofty, or comfortably narrow, not perfectly humane? If we do not feign when we say that we despise Folly, we shut the brain. There is a disdainful attitude in the presence of Folly, partaking of the foolishness to Comic perception: and anger is not much less foolish than disdain. The struggle we have to conduct is essence against essence. Let no one doubt of the sequel when this emanation of what is firmest in us is launched to strike down the daughter of Unreason and Sentimentalism: such being Folly's parentage, when it is respectable.

Our modern system of combating her is too long defensive, and carried on too ploddingly with concrete engines of war in the attack. She has time to get behind entrenchments. She is ready to stand a siege, before the heavily armed man of science and the writer of the leading article or elaborate essay have primed their big guns. It should be remembered that she has charms for the multitude; and an English multitude seeing her make a gallant fight of it will be half in love with her, certainly willing to lend her a cheer. Benevolent subscriptions assist her to hire her own man of science, her own organ in the Press. If ultimately she is cast out and overthrown, she can stretch a finger at gaps in our ranks. She can say that she commanded an army and seduced men, whom we thought sober men and safe, to act as her lieutenants. We learn rather gloomily, after she has flashed her lantern, that we have in our midst able men and men with minds for whom there is no pole-star in intellectual navigation. Comedy, or the Comic element, is the specific for the poison of delusion while Folly is passing from the state of vapour to substantial form.

O for a breath of Aristophanes, Rabelais, Voltaire, Cervantes, Fielding, Molière! These are spirits that, if you know them well, will come when you do call. You will find the very invocation of them act on you like a renovating air—the South-west coming off the sea, or a cry in the Alps.

No one would presume to say that we are deficient in jokers. They abound, and the organisation directing their machinery to shoot them in the wake of the leading article and the popular sentiment is good.

But the Comic differs from them in addressing the wits for laughter; and the sluggish wits want some training to respond to it, whether in public life or private, and particularly when the feelings are excited.

The sense of the Comic is much blunted by habits of punning and of using humouristic phrase: the trick of employing Johnsonian polysyllables to treat of the infinitely little. And it really may be humorous, of a kind, yet it will miss the point by going too much round about it.

A certain French Duke Pasquier died, some years back, at a very advanced age. He had been the venerable Duke Pasquier in his later years up to the period of his death. There was a report of Duke Pasquier that he was a man of profound egoism. Hence an argument arose, and was warmly sustained, upon the excessive selfishness of those who, in a world of troubles, and calls to action, and innumerable duties, husband their strength for the sake of living on. Can it be possible, the argument ran, for a truly generous heart to continue beating up to the age of a hundred? Duke Pasquier was not without his defenders, who likened him to the oak of the forest—a venerable comparison.

The argument was conducted on both sides with spirit and earnestness, lightened here and there by frisky touches of the polysyllabic playful, reminding one of the serious pursuit of their fun by truant boys, that are assured they are out of the eye of their master, and now and then indulge in an imitation of him. And well might it be supposed that the Comic idea was asleep, not overlooking them! It resolved at last to this, that either Duke Pasquier was a scandal on our humanity in clinging to life so long, or that he honoured it by so sturdy a resistance to the enemy. As one who has entangled himself in a labyrinth is glad to get out again at the entrance, the argument ran about to conclude with its commencement.

Now, imagine a master of the Comic treating this theme, and particularly the argument on it. Imagine an Aristophanic comedy of THE CENTENARIAN, with choric praises of heroical early death, and the same of a stubborn vitality, and the poet laughing at the chorus; and the grand question for contention in dialogue, as to the exact age when a man should die, to the identical minute, that he may preserve the respect of his fellows, followed by a systematic attempt to make an accurate measurement in parallel lines, with a tough rope-yarn by one party, and a string of yawns by the other, of the veteran's power of enduring life, and our capacity for enduring ***him***, with tremendous pulling on both sides.

Would not the Comic view of the discussion illumine it and the disputants like very lightning? There are questions, as well as persons, that only the Comic can fitly touch.

Aristophanes would probably have crowned the ancient tree, with the consolatory observation to the haggard line of long-expectant heirs of the Centenarian, that they live to see the blessedness of coming of a strong stock. The shafts of his ridicule would mainly have been aimed at the disputants. For the sole ground of the argument was the old man's character, and sophists are not needed to demonstrate that we can very soon have too much of a bad thing. A Centenarian does not necessarily provoke the Comic idea, nor does the corpse of a duke. It is not provoked in the order of nature, until we draw its penetrating attentiveness to some circumstance with which we have been mixing our private interests, or our speculative obfuscation. Dulness, insensible to the Comic, has the privilege of arousing it; and the laying of a dull finger on matters of human life is the surest method of establishing electrical communications with a battery of laughter—where the Comic idea is prevalent.

But if the Comic idea prevailed with us, and we had an Aristophanes to barb and wing it, we should be breathing air of Athens. Prosers now pouring forth on us like public fountains would be cut short in the street and left blinking, dumb as pillar-posts, with letters thrust into their mouths. We should throw off incubus, our dreadful familiar—by some called boredom—whom it is our present humiliation to be just alive enough to loathe, never quick enough to foil. There would be a bright and positive, clear Hellenic perception of facts. The vapours of Unreason and Sentimentalism would be blown away before they were productive. Where would Pessimist and Optimist be? They would in any case have a diminished audience. Yet possibly the change of despots, from good-natured old obtuseness to keen-edged intelligence, which is by nature merciless, would be more than we could bear. The rupture of the link between dull people, consisting in the fraternal agreement that something is too clever for them, and a shot beyond them, is not to be thought of lightly; for, slender though the link may seem, it is equivalent to a cement forming a concrete of dense cohesion, very desirable in the estimation of the statesman.

A political Aristophanes, taking advantage of his lyrical Bacchic licence, was found too much for political Athens. I would not ask to have him revived, but that the sharp light of such a spirit as his might be with us to strike now and then on public affairs, public themes, to make them spin along more briskly.

He hated with the politician's fervour the sophist who corrupted simplicity of thought, the poet who destroyed purity of style, the demagogue, 'the saw-toothed monster,' who, as he conceived, chicaned the mob, and he held his own against them by strength of laughter, until fines, the curtailing of his Comic licence in the chorus, and ultimately the ruin of Athens, which could no longer support the expense of the chorus, threw him altogether on dialogue, and brought him under the law. After the catastrophe, the poet, who had ever been gazing back at the men of Marathon and Salamis, must have felt that he had foreseen it; and that he was wise when he pleaded for peace, and derided military coxcombry, and the captious old creature Demus, we can admit. He had the Comic poet's gift of common-sense—which does not always include political intelligence; yet his political tendency raised him above the Old Comedy turn for uproarious farce. He abused Socrates, but Xenophon, the disciple of Socrates, by his trained rhetoric saved the Ten Thousand. Aristophanes might say that if his warnings had been followed there would have been no such thing as a mercenary Greek expedition under Cyrus. Athens, however, was on a landslip, falling; none could arrest it. To gaze back, to uphold the old times, was a most natural conservatism, and fruitless. The aloe had bloomed. Whether right or wrong in his politics and his criticisms, and bearing in mind the instruments he played on and the audience he had to win, there is an idea in his comedies: it is the Idea of Good Citizenship.

He is not likely to be revived. He stands, like Shakespeare, an unapproachable. Swift says of him, with a loving chuckle:

> 'But as for Comic Aristophanes,
> The dog too witty and too prófane is.'

Aristophanes was 'prófane,' under satiric direction, unlike his rivals Cratinus, Phrynichus, Ameipsias, Eupolis, and others, if we are to believe him, who in their extraordinary Donnybrook Fair of the day of Comedy, thumped one another and everybody else with absolute heartiness, as he did, but aimed at small game, and dragged forth particular women, which he did not. He is an aggregate of many men, all of a certain greatness. We may build up a conception of his powers if we mount Rabelais upon Hudibras, lift him with the songfulness of Shelley, give him a vein of Heinrich Heine, and cover him with the mantle of the Anti-Jacobin, adding (that there may be some Irish in him) a dash of Grattan, before he is in motion.

But such efforts at conceiving one great one by incorporation of minors are vain, and cry for excuse. Supposing Wilkes for leading man in a country constantly plunging into war under some plumed Lamachus, with enemies periodically firing the land up to the gates of London, and a Samuel Foote, of prodigious genius, attacking him with ridicule, I think it gives a notion of the conflict engaged in by Aristophanes. This laughing bald-pate, as he calls himself, was a Titanic pamphleteer, using laughter for his political weapon; a laughter without scruple, the laughter of Hercules. He was primed with wit, as with the garlic he speaks of giving to the game-cocks, to make them fight the better. And he was a lyric poet of aërial delicacy, with the homely song of a jolly national poet, and a poet of such feeling that the comic mask is at times no broader than a cloth on a face to show the serious features of our common likeness. He is not to be revived; but if his method were studied, some of the fire in him would come to us, and we might be revived.

Taking them generally, the English public are most in sympathy with this primitive Aristophanic comedy, wherein the comic is capped by the grotesque, irony tips the wit, and satire is a naked sword. They have the basis of the Comic in them: an esteem for common-sense. They cordially dislike the reverse of it. They have a rich laugh, though it is not the ***gros rire*** of the Gaul tossing ***gros sel***, nor the polished Frenchman's mentally digestive laugh. And if they have now, like a monarch with a troop of dwarfs, too many jesters kicking the dictionary about, to let them reflect that they are dull, occasionally, like the pensive monarch surprising himself with an idea of an idea of his own, they look so. And they are given to looking in the glass. They must see that something ails them. How much even the better order of them will endure, without a thought of the defensive, when the person afflicting them is protected from satire, we read in Memoirs of a Preceding Age, where the vulgarly tyrannous hostess of a great house of reception shuffled the guests and played them like a pack of cards, with her exact estimate of the strength of each one printed on them: and still this house continued to be the most popular in England; nor did the lady ever appear in print or on the boards as the comic type that she was.

It has been suggested that they have not yet spiritually comprehended the signification of living in society; for who are cheerfuller, brisker of wit, in the fields, and as explorers, colonisers, backwoodsmen? They are happy in rough exercise, and also in complete repose. The intermediate condition, when they are called upon to talk to one another, upon other than affairs of business or their hobbies, reveals them wearing a curious look of vacancy, as it were the socket of an eye wanting. The Comic is perpetually springing up in social life, and, it oppresses them from not being perceived.

Thus, at a dinner-party, one of the guests, who happens to have enrolled himself in a Burial Company, politely entreats the others to inscribe their names as shareholders, expatiating on the advantages accruing to them in the event of their very possible speedy death, the salubrity of the site, the aptitude of the soil for a quick consumption of their remains, etc.; and they drink sadness from the incongruous man, and conceive indigestion, not seeing him in a sharply defined light, that would bid them taste the comic of him. Or it is mentioned that a newly elected member of our Parliament celebrates his arrival at eminence by the publication of a book on cab-fares, dedicated to a beloved female relative deceased, and the comment on it is the word 'Indeed.' But, merely for a contrast, turn to a not uncommon scene of yesterday in the hunting-field, where a brilliant young rider, having broken his collar-bone, trots away very soon after, against medical interdict, half put together in splinters, to the most distant meet of his neighbourhood, sure of escaping his doctor, who is the first person he encounters. 'I came here purposely to avoid you,' says the patient. 'I came here purposely to take care of you,' says the doctor. Off they go, and come to a swollen brook. The patient clears it handsomely: the doctor tumbles in. All the field are alive with the heartiest relish of every incident and every cross-light on it; and dull would the man have been thought who had not his word to say about it when riding home.

In our prose literature we have had delightful Comic writers. Besides Fielding and Goldsmith, there is Miss Austen, whose Emma and Mr. Elton might walk straight into a comedy, were the plot arranged for them. Galt's neglected novels have some characters and strokes of shrewd comedy. In our poetic literature the comic is delicate and graceful above the touch of Italian and French. Generally, however, the English elect excel in satire, and they are noble humourists. The national disposition is for hard-hitting, with a moral purpose to sanction it; or for a rosy, sometimes a larmoyant, geniality, not unmanly in its verging upon tenderness, and with a singular attraction for thick-headedness, to decorate it with asses' ears and the most beautiful sylvan haloes. But the Comic is a different spirit.

You may estimate your capacity for Comic perception by being able to detect the ridicule of them you love, without loving them less: and more by being able to see yourself somewhat ridiculous in dear eyes, and accepting the correction their image of you proposes.

Each one of an affectionate couple may be willing, as we say, to die for the other, yet unwilling to utter the agreeable word at the right moment; but if the wits were sufficiently quick for them to perceive that they are in a comic situation, as affectionate couples must be when they quarrel, they would not wait for the moon or the almanac, or a Dorine, to bring back the flood-tide of tender feelings, that they should join hands and lips.

If you detect the ridicule, and your kindliness is chilled by it, you are slipping into the grasp of Satire.

If instead of falling foul of the ridiculous person with a satiric rod, to make him writhe and shriek aloud, you prefer to sting him under a semi-caress, by which he shall in his anguish be rendered dubious whether indeed anything has hurt him, you are an engine of Irony.

If you laugh all round him, tumble him, roll him about, deal him a smack, and drop a tear on him, own his likeness to you and yours to your neighbour, spare him as little as you shun, pity him as much as you expose, it is a spirit of Humour that is moving you.

The Comic, which is the perceptive, is the governing spirit, awakening and giving aim to these powers of laughter, but it is not to be confounded with them: it enfolds a thinner form of them, differing from satire, in not sharply driving into the quivering sensibilities, and from humour, in not comforting them and tucking them up, or indicating a broader than the range of this bustling world to them.

Fielding's Jonathan Wild presents a case of this peculiar distinction, when that man of eminent greatness remarks upon the unfairness of a trial in which the condemnation has been brought about by twelve men of the opposite party; for it is not satiric, it is not humorous; yet it is immensely comic to hear a guilty villain protesting that his own 'party' should have a voice in the Law. It opens an avenue into villains' ratiocination.[9] And the Comic is not cancelled though we should suppose Jonathan to be giving play to his humour. I may have dreamed this or had it suggested to me, for on referring to Jonathan Wild, I do not find it.

9. The exclamation of Lady Booby, when Joseph defends himself: 'Your virtue! I shall never survive it!' etc., is another instance.—Joseph Andrews. Also that of Miss Mathews in her narrative to Booth: 'But such are the friendships of women.'—Amelia.

Apply the case to the man of deep wit, who is ever certain of his condemnation by the opposite party, and then it ceases to be comic, and will be satiric.

The look of Fielding upon Richardson is essentially comic. His method of correcting the sentimental writer is a mixture of the comic and the humorous. Parson Adams is a creation of humour. But both the conception and the presentation of Alceste and of Tartuffe, of Célimène and Philaminte, are purely comic, addressed to the intellect: there is no humour in them, and they refresh the intellect they quicken to detect their comedy, by force of the contrast they offer between themselves and the wiser world about them; that is to say, society, or that assemblage of minds whereof the Comic spirit has its origin.

Byron had splendid powers of humour, and the most poetic satire that we have example of, fusing at times to hard irony. He had no strong comic sense, or he would not have taken an anti-social position, which is directly opposed to the Comic; and in his philosophy, judged by philosophers, he is a comic figure, by reason of this deficiency. 'So bald er philosophirt ist er ein Kind,' Goethe says of him. Carlyle sees him in this comic light, treats him in the humorous manner.

The Satirist is a moral agent, often a social scavenger, working on a storage of bile.

The Ironeïst is one thing or another, according to his caprice. Irony is the humour of satire; it may be savage as in Swift, with a moral object, or sedate, as in Gibbon, with a malicious. The foppish irony fretting to be seen, and the irony which leers, that you shall not mistake its intention, are failures in satiric effort pretending to the treasures of ambiguity.

The Humourist of mean order is a refreshing laugher, giving tone to the feelings and sometimes allowing the feelings to be too much for him. But the humourist of high has an embrace of contrasts beyond the scope of the Comic poet.

Heart and mind laugh out at Don Quixote, and still you brood on him. The juxtaposition of the knight and squire is a Comic conception, the opposition of their natures most humorous. They are as different as the two hemispheres in the time of Columbus, yet they touch and are bound in one by laughter. The knight's great aims and constant mishaps, his chivalrous valiancy exercised on absurd objects, his good sense along the highroad of the craziest of expeditions; the compassion he plucks out of derision, and the admirable figure he preserves while stalking through the frantically grotesque and burlesque assailing him, are in the loftiest moods of humour, fusing the Tragic sentiment with the Comic narrative.

The stroke of the great humourist is world-wide, with lights of Tragedy in his laughter.

Taking a living great, though not creative, humourist to guide our description: the skull of Yorick is in his hands in our seasons of festival; he sees visions of primitive man capering preposterously under the gorgeous robes of ceremonial. Our souls must be on fire when we wear solemnity, if we would not press upon his shrewdest nerve. Finite and infinite flash from one to the other with him, lending him a two-edged thought that peeps out of his peacefullest lines by fits, like the lantern of the fire-watcher at windows, going the rounds at night. The comportment and performances of men in society are to him, by the vivid comparison with their mortality, more grotesque than respectable. But ask yourself, Is he always to be relied on for justness? He will fly straight as the emissary eagle back to Jove at the true Hero. He will also make as determined a swift descent upon the man of his wilful choice, whom we cannot distinguish as a true one. This vast power of his, built up of the feelings and the intellect in union, is often wanting in proportion and in discretion. Humourists touching upon History or Society are given to be capricious. They are, as in the case of Sterne, given to be sentimental; for with them the feelings are primary, as with singers. Comedy, on the other hand, is an interpretation of the general mind, and is for that reason of necessity kept in restraint. The French lay marked stress on ***mesure et goût***, and they own how much they owe to Molière for leading them in simple justness and taste. We can teach them many things; they can teach us in this.

The Comic poet is in the narrow field, or enclosed square, of the society he depicts; and he addresses the still narrower enclosure of men's intellects, with reference to the operation of the social world upon their characters. He is not concerned with beginnings or endings or surroundings, but with what you are now weaving. To understand his work and value it, you must have a sober liking of your kind and a sober estimate of our civilized qualities. The aim and business of the Comic poet are misunderstood, his meaning is not seized nor his point of view taken, when he is accused of dishonouring our nature and being hostile to sentiment, tending to spitefulness and making an unfair use of laughter. Those who detect irony in Comedy do so because they choose to see it in life. Poverty, says the satirist, has nothing harder in itself than that it makes men ridiculous. But poverty is never ridiculous to Comic perception until it attempts to make its rags conceal its bareness in a forlorn attempt at decency, or foolishly to rival ostentation. Caleb Balderstone, in his endeavour to keep up the honour of a noble household in a state of beggary, is an exquisitely comic character. In the case of 'poor relatives,' on the other hand, it is the rich, whom they perplex, that are really comic; and to laugh at the former, not seeing the comedy of the latter, is to betray dulness of vision. Humourist and Satirist frequently hunt together as Ironeïsts in pursuit of the grotesque, to the exclusion of the Comic. That was an affecting moment in the history of the Prince Regent, when the First Gentleman of Europe burst into tears at a sarcastic remark of Beau Brummell's on the cut of his coat. Humour, Satire, Irony, pounce on it altogether as their common prey. The Comic spirit eyes but does not touch it. Put into action, it would be farcical. It is too gross for Comedy.

Incidents of a kind casting ridicule on our unfortunate nature instead of our conventional life, provoke derisive laughter, which thwarts the Comic idea. But derision is foiled by the play of the intellect. Most of doubtful causes in contest are open to Comic interpretation, and any intellectual pleading of a doubtful cause contains germs of an Idea of Comedy.

The laughter of satire is a blow in the back or the face. The laughter of Comedy is impersonal and of unrivalled politeness, nearer a smile; often no more than a smile. It laughs through the mind, for the mind directs it; and it might be called the humour of the mind.

One excellent test of the civilization of a country, as I have said, I take to be the flourishing of the Comic idea and Comedy; and the test of true Comedy is that it shall awaken thoughtful laughter.

If you believe that our civilization is founded in common-sense (and it is the first condition of sanity to believe it), you will, when contemplating men, discern a Spirit overhead; not more heavenly than the light flashed upward from glassy surfaces, but luminous and watchful; never shooting beyond them, nor lagging in the rear; so closely attached to them that it may be taken for a slavish reflex, until its features are studied. It has the sage's brows, and the sunny malice of a faun lurks at the corners of the half-closed lips drawn in an idle wariness of half tension. That slim feasting smile, shaped like the long-bow, was once a big round satyr's laugh, that flung up the brows like a fortress lifted by gunpowder. The laugh will come again, but it will be of the order of the smile, finely tempered, showing sunlight of the mind, mental richness rather than noisy enormity. Its common aspect is one of unsolicitous observation, as if surveying a full field and having leisure to dart on its chosen morsels, without any fluttering eagerness. Men's future upon earth does not attract it; their honesty and shapeliness in the present does; and whenever they wax out of proportion, overblown, affected, pretentious, bombastical, hypocritical, pedantic, fantastically delicate; whenever it sees them self-deceived or hoodwinked, given to run riot in idolatries, drifting into vanities, congregating in absurdities, planning short-sightedly, plotting dementedly; whenever they are at variance with their professions, and violate the unwritten but perceptible laws binding them in consideration one to another; whenever they offend sound reason, fair justice; are false in humility or mined with conceit, individually, or in the bulk—the Spirit overhead will look humanely malign and cast an oblique light on them, followed by volleys of silvery laughter. That is the Comic Spirit.

Not to distinguish it is to be bull-blind to the spiritual, and to deny the existence of a mind of man where minds of men are in working conjunction.

You must, as I have said, believe that our state of society is founded in common-sense, otherwise you will not be struck by the contrasts the Comic Spirit perceives, or have it to look to for your consolation. You will, in fact, be standing in that peculiar oblique beam of light, yourself illuminated to the general eye as the very object of chase and doomed quarry of the thing obscure to you. But to feel its presence and to see it is your assurance that many sane and solid minds are with you in what you are experiencing: and this of itself spares you the pain of satirical heat, and the bitter craving to strike heavy blows. You share the sublime of wrath, that would not have hurt the foolish, but merely demonstrate their foolishness. Molière was contented to revenge himself on the critics of the École des Femmes, by writing the Critique de l'École des Femmes, one of the wisest as well as the playfullest of studies in criticism. A perception of the comic spirit gives high fellowship. You become a citizen of the selecter world, the highest we know of in connection with our old world, which is not supermundane. Look there for your unchallengeable upper class! You feel that you are one of this our civilized community, that you cannot escape from it, and would not if you could. Good hope sustains you; weariness does not overwhelm you; in isolation you see no charms for vanity; personal pride is greatly moderated. Nor shall your title of citizenship exclude you from worlds of imagination or of devotion. The Comic spirit is not hostile to the sweetest songfully poetic. Chaucer bubbles with it: Shakespeare overflows: there is a mild moon's ray of it (pale with super-refinement through distance from our flesh and blood planet) in Comus. Pope has it, and it is the daylight side of the night half obscuring Cowper. It is only hostile to the priestly element, when that, by baleful swelling, transcends and overlaps the bounds of its office: and then, in extreme cases, it is too true to itself to speak, and veils the lamp: as, for example, the spectacle of Bossuet over the dead body of Molière: at which the dark angels may, but men do not laugh.

We have had comic pulpits, for a sign that the laughter-moving and the worshipful may be in alliance: I know not how far comic, or how much assisted in seeming so by the unexpectedness and the relief of its appearance: at least they are popular, they are said to win the ear. Laughter is open to perversion, like other good things; the scornful and the brutal sorts are not unknown to us; but the laughter directed by the Comic spirit is a harmless wine, conducing to sobriety in the degree that it enlivens. It enters you like fresh air into a study; as when one of the sudden contrasts of the comic idea floods the brain like reassuring daylight. You are cognizant of the true kind by feeling that you take it in, savour it, and have what flowers live on, natural air for food. That which you give out—the joyful roar—is not the better part; let that go to good fellowship and the benefit of the lungs. Aristophanes promises his auditors that if they will retain the ideas of the comic poet carefully, as they keep dried fruits in boxes, their garments shall smell odoriferous of wisdom throughout the year. The boast will not be thought an empty one by those who have choice friends that have stocked themselves according to his directions. Such treasuries of sparkling laughter are wells in our desert. Sensitiveness to the comic laugh is a step in civilization. To shrink from being an object of it is a step in cultivation. We know the degree of refinement in men by the matter they will laugh at, and the ring of the laugh; but we know likewise that the larger natures are distinguished by the great breadth of their power of laughter, and no one really loving Molière is refined by that love to despise or be dense to Aristophanes, though it may be that the lover of Aristophanes will not have risen to the height of Molière. Embrace them both, and you have the whole scale of laughter in your breast. Nothing in the world surpasses in stormy fun the scene in The Frogs, when Bacchus and Xanthias receive their thrashings from the hands of businesslike Œacus, to discover which is the divinity of the two, by his imperviousness to the mortal condition of pain, and each, under the obligation of not crying out, makes believe that his horrible bellow—the god's ***iou iou*** being the lustier—means only the stopping of a sneeze, or horseman sighted, or the prelude to an invocation to some deity: and the slave contrives that the god shall get the bigger lot of blows. Passages of Rabelais, one or two in Don Quixote, and the Supper in the Manner of the Ancients, in Peregrine Pickle, are of a similar cataract of laughter. But it is not illuminating; it is not the laughter of the mind. Molière's laughter, in his purest comedies, is ethereal, as light to our nature, as colour to our thoughts. The Misanthrope and the Tartuffe have no audible laughter; but the characters are steeped in the comic spirit. They quicken the mind through laughter, from coming out of the mind; and the mind accepts them because they are clear interpretations of certain chapters of the Book lying open before us all. Between these two stand Shakespeare and Cervantes, with the richer laugh of heart and mind in one; with much of the Aristophanic robustness, something of Molière's delicacy.

* * *

The laughter heard in circles not pervaded by the Comic idea, will sound harsh and soulless, like versified prose, if you step into them with a sense of the distinction. You will fancy you have changed your habitation to a planet remoter from the sun. You may be among powerful brains too. You will not find poets—or but a stray one, over-worshipped. You will find learned men undoubtedly, professors, reputed philosophers, and illustrious dilettanti. They have in them, perhaps, every element composing light, except the Comic. They read verse, they discourse of art; but their eminent faculties are not under that vigilant sense of a collective supervision, spiritual and present, which we have taken note of. They build a temple of arrogance; they speak much in the voice of oracles; their hilarity, if it does not dip in grossness, is usually a form of pugnacity.

Insufficiency of sight in the eye looking outward has deprived them of the eye that should look inward. They have never weighed themselves in the delicate balance of the Comic idea so as to obtain a suspicion of the rights and dues of the world; and they have, in consequence, an irritable personality. A very learned English professor crushed an argument in a political discussion, by asking his adversary angrily: 'Are you aware, sir, that I am a philologer?'

The practice of polite society will help in training them, and the professor on a sofa with beautiful ladies on each side of him, may become their pupil and a scholar in manners without knowing it: he is at least a fair and pleasing spectacle to the Comic Muse. But the society named polite is volatile in its adorations, and to-morrow will be petting a bronzed soldier, or a black African, or a prince, or a spiritualist: ideas cannot take root in its ever-shifting soil. It is besides addicted in self-defence to gabble exclusively of the affairs of its rapidly revolving world, as children on a whirligoround bestow their attention on the wooden horse or cradle ahead of them, to escape from giddiness and preserve a notion of identity. The professor is better out of a circle that often confounds by lionizing, sometimes annoys by abandoning, and always confuses. The school that teaches gently what peril there is lest a cultivated head should still be coxcomb's, and the collisions which may befall high-soaring minds, empty or full, is more to be recommended than the sphere of incessant motion supplying it with material.

Lands where the Comic spirit is obscure overhead are rank with raw crops of matter. The traveller accustomed to smooth highways and people not covered with burrs and prickles is amazed, amid so much that is fair and cherishable, to come upon such curious barbarism. An Englishman paid a visit of admiration to a professor in the Land of Culture, and was introduced by him to another distinguished professor, to whom he took so cordially as to walk out with him alone one afternoon. The first professor, an erudite entirely worthy of the sentiment of scholarly esteem prompting the visit, behaved (if we exclude the dagger) with the vindictive jealousy of an injured Spanish beauty. After a short prelude of gloom and obscure explosions, he discharged upon his faithless admirer the bolts of passionate logic familiar to the ears of flighty caballeros:—'Either I am a fit object of your admiration, or I am not. Of these things one—either you are competent to judge, in which case I stand condemned by you; or you are incompetent, and therefore impertinent, and you may betake yourself to your country again, hypocrite!' The admirer was for persuading the wounded scholar that it is given to us to be able to admire two professors at a time. He was driven forth.

Perhaps this might have occurred in any country, and a comedy of The Pedant, discovering the greedy humanity within the dusty scholar, would not bring it home to one in particular. I am mindful that it was in Germany, when I observe that the Germans have gone through no comic training to warn them of the sly, wise emanation eyeing them from aloft, nor much of satirical. Heinrich Heine has not been enough to cause them to smart and meditate. Nationally, as well as individually, when they are excited they are in danger of the grotesque, as when, for instance, they decline to listen to evidence, and raise a national outcry because one of German blood has been convicted of crime in a foreign country. They are acute critics, yet they still wield clubs in controversy. Compare them in this respect with the people schooled in La Bruyère, La Fontaine, Molière; with the people who have the figures of a Trissotin and a Vadius before them for a comic warning of the personal vanities of the caressed professor. It is more than difference of race. It is the difference of traditions, temper, and style, which comes of schooling.

The French controversialist is a polished swordsman, to be dreaded in his graces and courtesies. The German is Orson, or the mob, or a marching army, in defence of a good case or a bad—a big or a little. His irony is a missile of terrific tonnage: sarcasm he emits like a blast from a dragon's mouth. He must and will be Titan. He stamps his foe underfoot, and is astonished that the creature is not dead, but stinging; for, in truth, the Titan is contending, by comparison, with a god.

When the Germans lie on their arms, looking across the Alsatian frontier at the crowds of Frenchmen rushing to applaud L'ami Fritz at the Théâtre Français, looking and considering the meaning of that applause, which is grimly comic in its political response to the domestic moral of the play when the Germans watch and are silent, their force of character tells. They are kings in music, we may say princes in poetry, good speculators in philosophy, and our leaders in scholarship. That so gifted a race, possessed moreover of the stern good sense which collects the waters of laughter to make the wells, should show at a disadvantage, I hold for a proof, instructive to us, that the discipline of the comic spirit is needful to their growth. We see what they can reach to in that great figure of modern manhood, Goethe. They are a growing people; they are conversable as well; and when their men, as in France, and at intervals at Berlin tea-tables, consent to talk on equal terms with their women, and to listen to them, their growth will be accelerated and be shapelier. Comedy, or in any form the Comic spirit, will then come to them to cut some figures out of the block, show them the mirror, enliven and irradiate the social intelligence.

Modern French comedy is commendable for the directness of the study of actual life, as far as that, which is but the early step in such a scholarship, can be of service in composing and colouring the picture. A consequence of this crude, though well-meant, realism is the collision of the writers in their scenes and incidents, and in their characters. The Muse of most of them is an ***Aventurière***. She is clever, and a certain diversion exists in the united scheme for confounding her. The object of this person is to reinstate herself in the decorous world; and either, having accomplished this purpose through deceit, she has a ***nostalgie de la boue***, that eventually casts her back into it, or she is exposed in her course of deception when she is about to gain her end. A very good, innocent young man is her victim, or a very astute, goodish young man obstructs her path. This latter is enabled to be the champion of the decorous world by knowing the indecorous well. He has assisted in the progress of Aventurières downward; he will not help them to ascend. The world is with him; and certainly it is not much of an ascension they aspire to; but what sort of a figure is he? The triumph of a candid realism is to show him no hero. You are to admire him (for it must be supposed that realism pretends to waken some admiration) as a credibly living young man; no better, only a little firmer and shrewder, than the rest. If, however, you think at all, after the curtain has fallen, you are likely to think that the Aventurières have a case to plead against him. True, and the author has not said anything to the contrary; he has but painted from the life; he leaves his audience to the reflections of unphilosophic minds upon life, from the specimen he has presented in the bright and narrow circle of a spy-glass.

I do not know that the fly in amber is of any particular use, but the Comic idea enclosed in a comedy makes it more generally perceptible and portable, and that is an advantage. There is a benefit to men in taking the lessons of Comedy in congregations, for it enlivens the wits; and to writers it is beneficial, for they must have a clear scheme, and even if they have no idea to present, they must prove that they have made the public sit to them before the sitting to see the picture. And writing for the stage would be a corrective of a too-incrusted scholarly style, into which some great ones fall at times. It keeps minor writers to a definite plan, and to English. Many of them now swelling a plethoric market, in the composition of novels, in pun-manufactories and in journalism; attached to the machinery forcing perishable matter on a public that swallows voraciously and groans; might, with encouragement, be attending to the study of art in literature. Our critics appear to be fascinated by the quaintness of our public, as the world is when our beast-garden has a new importation of magnitude, and the creatures appetite is reverently consulted. They stipulate for a writer's popularity before they will do much more than take the position of umpires to record his failure or success. Now the pig supplies the most popular of dishes, but it is not accounted the most honoured of animals, unless it be by the cottager. Our public might surely be led to try other, perhaps finer, meat. It has good taste in song. It might be taught as justly, on the whole, and the sooner when the cottager's view of the feast shall cease to be the humble one of our literary critics, to extend this capacity for delicate choosing in the direction of the matter arousing laughter.

ALL ABOUT ALGAE
A Window in Thrums
J M Barrie
Betty Zane
Zane Grey
Dona Perfecta
MARIANELA
El abuelo
Book of Meditations
James Allen
The Lady of the Mount
My Lady Nicotine
J. M. Barrie
What Every Woman Knows
J M Barrie
Auld Licht Idylls
J M Barrie
We
Jules Verne
EIGHT HUNDRED LEAGUES ON THE AMAZON
The Great Lakes
Peter and Wendy
J.M. BARRIE
White Fang
Jack London